SEBASTIAN ON GUARD!

Peering through the glass door of the locked museum, Sebastian could see the dark figure skulking toward the far wing, the one with the prehistoric exhibits. If only he could get to the roof, perhaps Sebastian could see who was inside and what he—or she—was doing. He scurried around the side to the fire escape and edged his way up the metal steps. His stomach churned. Heights were not his favorite place—after all, he wasn't a bird dog.

Sebastian bellied up to the skylight and peered down.

The dark figure was near the woolly mammoth. Long boxes were spread around the floor. Was someone stealing the woolly mammoth?

Bantam Skylark Books by Mary Blount Christian
Ask your bookseller for the books you have missed

MARY BLOUNT CHRISTIAN

SEBASTIAN
(Super Sleuth)
and the
Bone to Pick Mystery

ILLUSTRATED BY LISA McCUE

A BANTAM SKYLARK BOOK®
TORONTO · NEW YORK · LONDON · SYDNEY · AUCKLAND

RL 5, 008–011

SEBASTIAN (SUPER SLEUTH) AND THE BONE TO PICK MYSTERY
*A Bantam Book / published by arrangement with
Macmillan Publishing Company*

PRINTING HISTORY
*Macmillan edition published September 1983
Bantam Skylark edition / April 1986*

Skylark Books is a registered trademark of Bantam Books, Inc.
Registered in U.S. Patent and Trademark Office and elsewhere.

ISBN 0-553-15385-4

Published simultaneously in the United States and Canada

*Bantam Books are published by Bantam Books, Inc. Its trade-
mark, consisting of the words "Bantam Books" and the por-
trayal of a rooster, is Registered in U.S. Patent and Trademark
Office and in other countries. Marca Registrada, Bantam
Books, Inc., 666 Fifth Avenue, New York, New York 10103.*

PRINTED IN THE UNITED STATES OF AMERICA
CW   0 9 8 7 6 5 4 3 2

Contents

1
It's a Dog's Life

Sebastian scowled at his master. John Quincy Jones lay sprawled across the entire length of the couch, reading the Sunday newspaper. Did he *have* to take up the whole thing? What was a dog to do?

With a heavy sigh, Sebastian dropped to the thick rug. He flung all four feet into the air, rolling and moaning contentedly as all the itchy parts responded. *Ummmm.*

This was the life. Two bachelors sharing a dangerous job five days a week, and sharing the small but comfortable apartment the rest of the time.

John was the only one who was actually *paid* for his work as a detective with the city police force. But Sebastian (Super Sleuth) felt he, the incomparable canine, did most of the work. Yessir, the old hairy hawkshaw really earned his keep, relying on his expertise as a master of disguise, his incredibly keen mind, and his fantastic nose to sniff out clues.

And little enough thanks he got for it, too! he thought. He let his huge paws drop with a plop—*Oooof!*—on the floor and lay on his side, panting from the effort.

Sebastian yawned. Yes, this bachelor life was the perfect answer for the dynamic dog, Sebastian the swashbuckler. And for John, who was okay—for a human.

He felt a slight prickle behind his ear and rolled over to swipe a big paw in that general direction. His eye fell on an interesting picture in the news-

paper John held. It was a picture of the biggest bone he'd ever seen in his life. He drooled hungrily.

Fortunately, reading was among Sebastian's many hidden talents, so he leaned forward to see the fine print.

A Professor Harbart Idelmann had discovered the jawbone of a woolly mammoth on the outskirts of the city, the story said. He was given a large grant of money to try to find the rest of it.

Imagine! Sebastian thought. Humans getting money to do something as much fun as digging up bones! Why, that should be its own reward.

He blinked sleepily and climbed onto one end of the couch, wiggling and nudging until John drew up his legs and gave him more room.

He had just dozed off with visions of mammoth bones in his head when the phone jarred him awake.

John yawned and pulled it to him, moaning a lazy hello into it. Sebastian was just settling back when John suddenly sat up to attention.

"Mother!" he all but screamed. "You're—where? You're—what? Of course—I'd love to see you some-time soon. Now? I can hardly wait—heh, heh. See you, Mother."

John slammed the phone into its cradle and jerked at the paper under Sebastian, sending the old super sleuth scrambling to the floor. "Get up! Out of the way, old fellow. Oh, good grief, look at this place. You left fur on the couch!"

Of course he left fur on the couch! What did John want him to do—lick it off like some stupid cat and come up with a hairball? What was the matter with him? Sebastian settled on his haunches and watched his master run around like a madman, scooping up newspapers and dirty glasses and snack plates as he went.

Dishes clattered in the kitchen as John slammed them into the dishwasher and turned it on with a whir. He grabbed a feather duster and dashed into the small living room, hurriedly swiping it over the furniture.

That phone call sure put John in some sort of fret, Sebastian concluded. He wondered what sort of lady John's mother was.

Well, he'd help out all he could. He trotted into the bedroom and found a couple of stale crackers with some hardened cheese on a plate by John's bed. He flicked out his tongue and sucked them in, swallowing quickly. There. That should be enough. John could handle the rest. He stepped up on the bed, circling to make himself comfortable.

But John swept through the door, snatching underwear from the chair and shoving it into a

4

drawer. "Get down, Sebastian. Off!" John shouted. He threw the bedcovers across the bed and smoothed them rapidly.

Sebastian sat watching, nose indignantly in the air, while John tried to do a month's worth of housekeeping in only a few minutes.

The doorbell sounded. John swallowed hard. "Wouldn't you know there wouldn't be enough traffic today to slow her taxi even a little?" he muttered. He pushed past Sebastian toward the door.

In his four years of working with John on the police force Sebastian had never seen his master in such a state of panic. Well, he'd stood by John in some pretty sticky situations—The Mystery of Who Put the Ham in Hamlet and The Secret of the Salty Sea Dog, to name just two. But who was counting? He'd stand by him now.

Besides, he was more curious than a cat about the object of John's panic. He trotted behind John into the living room to see for himself.

John suddenly stared at Sebastian as if he were seeing him for the first time. "Oh, my gosh!" he groaned. "What will Mother think about you *inside* the house?"

John took a deep breath and opened the front door. "Mother! How good to see you!"

A woman in a brown fur coat—how *could* she?
—and a hat that looked like a bowl of flowers set
down a brocade suitcase. She threw one arm
around John. "John darling," she cooed, running
her free hand over the hall table to leave a track in
the dust. She frowned. "Oh, dear—you do need a
woman's touch," she said.

"Don't worry, John dear. We'll have this place
in shape in no time," she went on, flicking off her
coat. She spotted Sebastian. *Ode d'Eiffel Tower*
rushed at his nostrils as she leaned closer, her
mouth agape.

"It's one thing to own and work with a dog. But
to allow him *in the house*? Dogs are—are messy
and they shed! John, you *know* you're allergic to
dogs," she said.

"But, I'm not, Mother!" John argued. "I—achooo!
—don't know how you ever thought that!"

"See, dear? You're sneezing now! Mothers always
know best."

Sebastian glared at her. Still, he thought he'd
better be on his best dog behavior. He was a continental canine, after all—Sebastian the Suave. He
knew how to get to humans. He sat on his haunches
and offered his paw.

But she'd already left in a whiff of perfume to
inspect the apartment, like a new colonel at an

army camp. "Now, I *know* you'll be disappointed, but I can stay no more than a *week*, John dear. I was on one of my little trips to the Bahamas, and I simply *must* hurry home with a million things to do—the theater board meetings, the art guild—you know." She dusted the lamp with Sebastian's favorite tug-of-war rag. "So none of your begging, dearest. It'll do you no good."

John smiled weakly. "You—you're not just passing through, Mother?" he asked. His shoulders sagged. "How—how wonderful."

Sebastian sank into a heap on the rug. That meant *she* would have the bed. And that meant John would take over the couch. So who would be out of a place to sleep? He, Sebastian (Super Sleuth) —that was who! It was a dog-eat-dog world.

Mrs. Jones patted the couch vigorously. A puff of dust and dog hair rose. She shook her head in disgust. "Well, no matter. We'll have this place shipshape before Maude comes to dinner tomorrow."

John sagged against a chair. "Maude? Dinner?"

"She's the most marvelous young lady who sat next to me on the tour bus in the Bahamas. We rode the same plane back," Mrs. Jones said. "Maude Culpepper. Why, she lives right here in the city." She pulled a bone from between the couch cushions, where Sebastian had put it for safekeeping.

7

"I've told her all about you. I want you to meet her. She's so sweet! She reminds me of myself at that age." Mrs. Jones dropped the bone into the waste can with a clunk.

Sebastian groaned, Uh-oh. She's hand-picked someone for John, and that spells trouble. Next thing you know, she'll be wagging some lady dog over here to meet *me*. Can't she see we don't *want* to get married, we're married to our work?

The phone rang. John answered, listening. "I have to go to work right now, Chief? No, that's all right, really! Right away, Chief. And Chief, *thank* you."

John slammed the phone into its cradle and rushed into the bedroom. He grabbed his coat. "Sorry, Mother, I'm needed at work," he explained. "We'll talk later. Make yourself at home." He kissed her cheek lightly. "Bye," he called as he pulled the front door open.

Before John could close it Sebastian pushed past him and trotted toward the car. No way was he going to stay there under her critical and un-sympathetic eye. Allergic, indeed. Humph! With a little luck maybe they'd be on this case all week.

"John dear, do be careful!" he heard Mrs. Jones call after them. "You forgot your raincoat and galoshes—and your sou'wester! It's going to rain."

8

John groaned as he opened the car door. "It's easier to take them than to argue her down," he said, trotting back to the apartment.

Sebastian scowled. Just "John dear"? No "Sebastian, be careful"?

It didn't matter. Look out, criminal world! he thought. Sebastian the Steadfast is on the prowl! He wagged the stump of his tail in anticipation.

He could hardly wait to find out what mystery lay ahead to challenge his master mind.

2
A Bone of Contention

Chief was pacing his office floor when Sebastian and John got to the police station. "Why'd you bring that fleabag here?" he demanded.

Sebastian decided to ignore Chief's rudeness and look for something good to eat instead. Chief was always on a diet. That didn't mean he didn't eat good stuff, though. It only meant he kept it hidden from sight.

Sebastian's adept nose told him to look around the potted palm tree in the corner.

"What's up, Chief?" John asked the beetle-browed boss.

"I had a call from Whirter MacMahan this morning, and he was really upset," Chief said.

The canine cop perked up his ears. Whirter MacMahan. The name sounded familiar. Wasn't he the curator of the Bosworthington Museum?

"He's the curator of the Bosworthington Museum," Chief said.

The museum, Sebastian mused. Just the right atmosphere for a dilettante dog, a dabbler in the arts. How nice to stroll among the Rembrandts and Van Goghs. He sniffed once, twice, then found the strongest scent of a prune danish among the leaves of Chief's potted palm.

"So what's his problem, Chief?" John asked.

"He says that last night the museum was broken into. I thought you should get over there before it opens to the public at one P.M. According to MacMahan there are some muddy prints around. The lab boys are there now. They'll try and get a make on the footprints."

"Come on, Sebastian," John called. "Here, boy."

Sebastian snapped the danish from its resting spot and swallowed it whole.

"Hey!" Chief yelled. "That dog—"

"—saved you from a wicked pastry lurking among your plants," John said, chuckling. "Who would have put it there to tempt a dieting man?"

Chief cleared his throat and blushed.

Sebastian knew that John realized as well as he: Chief had put the danish roll there. He didn't want anyone to know he had trouble dieting. Satisfied, Sebastian trotted out, licking his whiskers. He did wish Chief would buy his pastry at a better bakery —this was a tiny bit stale. He caught up with John and leaped into the car for the short drive to the museum. He hoped the museum coffee shop would be open today. Stale danish always made him hungry.

At the museum door John rang. He held his badge up to the glass door so the man inside could see it.

The man nodded and opened the door. "But he's got to stay outside. No dogs allowed," he said, nodding toward Sebastian.

Sebastian curled his lip in disgust. Deny the old super sleuth the run of the place? Cut him off from the clues? Nobody stops the dynamic dog! Sebastian promised himself. Was he not a master of disguise? A canine chameleon? He'd simply use his cunning at disguise.

When John and the man were out of sight, Sebastian dashed back to the car. There was John's raincoat and galoshes and sou'wester. Not as imaginative as the scuba gear in The Mystery of the Salty Sea Dog or the airline attendant in The Secret of the Skewered Skier, but it'd have to do in an emergency. He glanced at the clock on the car dash. It was nearly time for the museum to open. Well, that would save him further deceit—he'd just go in as an ordinary visitor.

The clandestine canine wiggled under the raincoat. He looked rather dashing with the raincoat thrown casually over his shoulders, he thought. The dapper dog slid into the sou'wester. Its wide brim would hide his fine crop of whiskers nicely. He jammed his hind legs into the galoshes and dashed back to the museum as the guard unlocked the door.

The guard swung the door open for Sebastian,

laughing. "Your mommy must've dressed you this morning. I can always tell. Mothers seem to have a sixth sense about rain, don't they? Heh, heh."

Rrrrrr, Sebastian replied as he slipped inside.

"Don't get grouchy with me, Mister!" the guard grumbled. "She ain't *my* mother!"

Sebastian dashed down the hall and sniffed. John's scent led to the west wing.

He trotted over to the west wing and pretended to be studying a piece of sculpture. Sunshine poured through a skylight onto the big sphere with a hole in it. It was called *People Walking*.

Humph! Sebastian thought, poking his nose through the hole. Where are the people and where are they walking?

He saw John talking to a man and strolled over closer to stand by a square block called *Bear on the Loose* so he could listen.

The man patted his pockets. "Now where did I put that pipe?" he said. "Oh, I wish I remembered things better."

"Can you show me where the burglar broke in?" John asked.

"I didn't find *any* place, actually. There are no signs of breaking and entering," the man replied.

"Then, was the museum left unlocked? Or was the burglary during visitor hours?" John asked.

15

"Certainly not!" the man replied. "I may be a tad forgetful, but I've *never* forgotten to lock up, I assure you. And we have guards everywhere when it is open."

"How many people have keys to the Bosworthington Museum?" John asked.

The man, still patting his pockets in search of his pipe, said, "Oh, just me—no, no—me and my wife. She started keeping one when I forgot and locked mine inside one time. Just the two of us, though."

"May I see your key, sir?" John said. "I'd like to see if it looks as if someone has made a recent copy of it—you know, telltale putty for an impression, or perhaps scrape marks."

"Ummm," the man said. "Ummm, now where— oh, here." He handed John a key. Sebastian leaned forward to get a good look. As far as he could see, it hadn't been tampered with.

"Ummm," John said, turning it over in his hands. "As far as I can see it hasn't been tampered with. I will want to talk to your wife and examine her key, of course."

The man nodded absently, turning his pockets inside out. "She's a journalist. She's on an assignment right now, but you could track her down at the dig, I think."

"The dig?" John asked.

16

"Yes, Professor Idelmann's dig on the outskirts of the city. My wife's doing an article on his search for the mammoth bones."

John's eyes brightened. "Oh—Marlena MacNulty MacMahan, the famous writer—of course!"

Sebastian remembered seeing her byline in some of the big magazines at home. If she was at the dig, that meant he and John would go there, too! He wiggled in anticipation. All those lovely big bones, just for the digging!

"I'll see her next," John told the man. "Right now, I'd like you to show me a list of what was taken and, of course, the footprints."

The man—who Sebastian cleverly concluded was Whirter MacMahan—spotted his pipe sitting on a sculpture called *The Garden* and grabbed it, stuffing it into his pocket. "Nothing was taken," he said.

"Then wh—" John asked.

"I can't find anything missing," Whirter Mac-Mahan said. "Actually, to tell the truth, we think someone got in here before—several days ago. We didn't call the police then because nothing was stolen and we weren't sure. But a second time? I don't like someone running around here willy-nilly. They may plan to steal something later."

"I can understand that," John said. "Did the police lab get samples of the footprints?"

"Yes, I suppose so," Mr. MacMahan replied. "But I'm afraid they weren't too clear—mostly just clumps of mud in the prehistoric section."

John and Mr. MacMahan went to the prehistoric collection in the south wing. Sebastian ambled along, skulking behind sculptures so they wouldn't notice him.

"I guess with a second woolly mammoth skeleton in town my exhibit of fossils won't be so spectacular," Mr. MacMahan said. "Of course, we have many other rare and expensive exhibits besides that!" he added, with obvious pride.

Sebastian gazed longingly at the giant bones bathed in sunlight from the skylight directly overhead. Doggie heaven must be something like this, he thought.

"I guess that'll teach us not to laugh at the man's ideas, no matter how silly they sound at the time," Mr. MacMahan told John.

"Laugh at him?" John asked. "About what?"

"Professor Idelmann wrote a book about this area being an old mammoth burial ground. He was all but laughed off the college campus where he teaches. The warehouse had stacks and stacks of his books gathering dust. But with this new find, his book is selling rapidly. And, of course, his position at the college is secured, too."

Sebastian leaned close to one of the bones and flicked out his tongue. Bluchk! It was as hard as stone and just about as tasty!

Sebastian had seen pictures of a woolly mammoth in a book before. This stack of bones must be what one looked like without its fur on. But what held all those bones together? And how did anybody know *how* to put them together?

He squinted at the bones. Tiny almost invisible wires were run through tiny holes in the bones, stringing them together. Each bone had a number on it, probably so someone would know which bone should be attached where. It was like painting by numbers, but with wire and bones!

"See?" Whirter MacMahan told John. "Here are the tracks. Next to the gentleman in the raincoat."

Sebastian waited until John and Mr. MacMahan left by the west hall, then he sniffed the tracks. Nothing too extraordinary. Just a little red mud. The print was smudged. It might be either a man with a small foot or a woman with a big one.

The old super sleuth filed his clues away in his steel-trap mind as he dashed down the east hall to avoid John and Whirter MacMahan. He pushed through the entrance and dashed to the car, shedding John's galoshes, sou'wester, and raincoat quickly.

John climbed in, glancing back at the rumpled raincoat with blobs of white fur still clinging to it.

"Honestly, Sebastian, why must you sleep on my coat? Look at all that—achoo!—fur on it."

"Oh well," he said, starting the engine. "We're off to the dig. Professor Idelmann's project should be to your liking!" John chuckled.

Sebastian wagged the stump of his tail. He certainly hoped the clues—and the bones—would be a whole lot meatier at the dig!

3
No Bones About It!

At the dig Sebastian lifted his nose excitedly and sniffed. Ahh, the smell of fresh-turned earth. And the smell of—of ham and cheese sandwiches?

The people working at the dig had stopped for lunch.

He leaped from the car behind John and trotted over to the tent, where the professor, a few students, and a woman—probably Marlena MacNulty Mac-Mahan—sat with sandwiches and chips.

John introduced himself. "And this is Sebastian," he added.

Marlena MacNulty MacMahan gave Sebastian a scratch under the chin that made his back leg thump. "Lunch?" she asked. Unfortunately, it was John she was asking.

John pulled up a campstool and sat down. Sebastian eased up to the picnic table and rested on his haunches, his eye on a slice of cheese that lay there unclaimed.

"Dug up anything interesting today?" John asked the professor.

"I expect to, any moment. In fact, I'm so sure that I've invited the press here this afternoon. You may stay and watch, if you wish."

"Thanks, but I'm on a case," John replied. "In fact, I only came by to take a look at Marlena MacNulty MacMahan's key to the museum."

"My key to the museum!" she exclaimed. "But whatever for?"

"I need to see if you still have it, and if you do, if it's been tampered with in any way," John said.

"My purse is over there," she said, rising. "I'll get it."

"Never mind," Professor Idelmann said, gently pushing her back. "I'll get it for you."

Sebastian had watched the piece of cheese as long as he could. With a flick of the tongue he scooped it into his mouth and swallowed it.

"Here you are, my dear," Professor Idelmann said, handing Marlena MacNulty MacMahan a gaping leather purse. "Now if you gentlemen and lady will excuse me, I see the rest of the press is arriving."

He trotted off with his hand extended and a hearty grin plastered across his face.

Marlena MacNulty MacMahan rummaged through her purse, which was brimming with pens, pencils, several notebooks, and an assortment of makeup. She pulled out a single key on a chain and handed it to John.

John examined Marlena MacNulty MacMahan's key to the Bosworthington Museum while the professor directed the television cameras to a spot close by his current excavation.

Sebastian kept his radar ears tuned to John's conversation with Marlena MacNulty MacMahan while he watched the professor.

"As you can see, the key to the museum is on a separate key ring from my car and house keys. I don't even have to pull it out unless Whirter locks his inside, poor forgetful dear."

"I can't see that your key has been tampered with," John told her. "Have you misplaced it at all lately?"

Marlena MacNulty MacMahan shook her head. "My purse stays right with me—or close by. As you can see, the key is right there."

John sighed. "I suppose that would have been too easy a solution. A puzzling situation."

Puzzling, indeed, Sebastian thought. What if Whirter MacMahan was trying to make it look as if someone had broken into the museum? What if he planned on stealing some of the expensive exhibits later? By pretending someone had broken in earlier, maybe he hoped to throw people off his trail. Other detectives might fall for that trick. But not Sebastian (Super Sleuth) and his sidekick, John Quincy Jones! Whirter MacMahan would bear watching.

In the distance thunder rumbled. Could Mrs. Jones be right about the rain? Sebastian wondered. How embarrassing.

The professor strutted back and forth in a knee-deep hole, advising the photographers on the best angles to take his picture while he was digging up the bone. He passed out autographed copies of his book to the reporters.

"Everyone laughed when I sat down to write my theory," he said. "But I showed them! I've shown everybody—and I predict that, even while your cameras are grinding away, I will find another bone to fit this fascinating prehistoric jigsaw puzzle."

He waved one of the cameras a little to the right, then leaned over to dig. Sebastian trotted over closer to the hole.

There was something about fresh-turned earth that he just could not resist. Sebastian leaped into the hole and scratched at the surface with all fours. Red dirt sprayed into the cameras and sent people scrambling.

"Stop!" the professor yelled. "Stop, dog! Stop your cameras, everyone. Stop!"

But the fresh-smelling dirt beckoned to him. Sebastian *couldn't* stop digging. And the cameras *wouldn't* stop rolling. Sebastian's claws hit something solid. He tugged at it.

"Let go!" the professor yelled. "That's mine! Let go!"

Sebastian *wanted* to let go! Really he did. But his canine tooth hung in a tiny hole in the bone, and the harder the professor tugged the more frantically Sebastian tugged, too. At last Sebastian worked the bone loose and relinquished it to the fuming professor.

Blushing, Sebastian sat back on his haunches and offered John his paw, whimpering an apology. But his master was really angry this time.

The professor, regaining his pompous composure, clutched the bone to himself. "If you will destroy that footage and reshoot," he told the television people, "I will do a reenactment of my finding the bone."

One of them laughed. "Are you kidding? This is the best thing that could possibly have happened. What a riot! Dig Goes to the Dogs! I can just see the headline now."

"I'm really sorry," John apologized to Professor

25

Idelmann. "I don't know what came over Sebastian. I guess it was just the sight of such a large bone that made him do it. He *is* a *dog*, you know."

The professor's face was red with rage. "That dog *ruined* my press conference. He made a laughing-stock out of me," he said, fuming.

Sebastian eased down and put his chin on his paws. How humble did a dog have to look before he could be forgiven?

"But you've found your third bone!" John reminded Professor Idelmann. "Doesn't that prove that it wasn't just a lucky find—that your theory was correct?"

The professor calmed down. "Ummm, well. I shall have to speed up my discoveries, I think, to overcome this bad publicity."

He clutched the bone to himself and stalked off toward Marlena MacNulty MacMahan. Sebastian rolled onto his back and covered his eyes with his paws. He wanted John to know how sorry he was.

John shook his head in disgust. "You old obedience school dropout—how could you?"

Sebastian shook off his momentary guilt. It wasn't his fault—he was a victim of his species! He trotted back to the tent to see if there were any lunch leftovers. Eating sometimes helps overcome unhappiness, he told himself.

While he was wolfing down a bag of chips and the sandwich crusts someone had left, Sebastian saw the professor stick the new bone into a box lined with straw.

"Two bones do not a woolly mammoth make. You still haven't proven that these suburban spots are an old woolly mammoth burial ground, as you said in your book," Marlena MacNulty MacMahan told him.

Professor Idelmann scowled at Marlena Mac-Nulty MacMahan. "I won't be made a fool of," he told her. "I'll show them all!" Suddenly he broke into his grin, the same one he gave to the news people earlier. "Believe me, before long I will have the whole woolly mammoth."

Rain spattered against the tent canvas. Mrs. Jones had been right.

"Would you mind terribly continuing the interview at dinner this evening?" the professor asked Marlena MacNulty MacMahan. "I'm so upset, I feel I need a sumptuous meal to calm me."

Sebastian licked his whiskers. If the professor ate to forget, maybe he wasn't all bad!

"I suppose that is all right, professor," Marlena MacNulty MacMahan said. "Whirter has a dinner tonight with several of the board members of the Bosworthington Museum and some letters to catch up on at home."

"I feel like La Maison Française tonight," Professor Idelmann said. "How does that sound to you?"

Sebastian curled his lip. How could someone with the good taste to like La Maison Française not adore the old super sleuth, the continental canine, the gourmet of dogdom? If Marlena MacNulty MacMahan was going to have dinner at La Maison Française, then he, Sebastian (Super Sleuth), would have to make the ultimate sacrifice and eat there, too. After all, she was a suspect. She was married to Whirter MacMahan, the museum director. Maybe she was going to help him steal something valuable. What if her journalism career were not as good as people thought? Maybe she thought she could liven it up with an exclusive story about a museum theft. She bears watching, too! Sebastian thought. And he couldn't think of a better place to start watching her than at La Maison Française— tonight. All in the line of duty, of course.

He licked his whiskers in eager anticipation.

4
The Dogged Maitre d'

John's anger at Sebastian seemed to dwindle as they got closer to home. It was replaced by anxiety. "I dread seeing the apartment, old boy," John confessed. "Mother loves to clean. When I was little, I couldn't even hide my socks under the bed like the other kids. And she never could understand that I liked my toys all out on the floor where I could see them." John chuckled.

Poor John, Sebastian thought. He had no idea what a terrible childhood he'd had! The compassionate canine vowed to be more thoughtful of his master from now on.

John brought his car to a stop outside the apartment and opened the door. Rain splattered the sidewalk. Sebastian dashed for his doggie door and pushed through. He skidded to a stop and shook hard, sending water droplets in every direction.

Almost instantly Mrs. Jones was right behind him, dabbing at the water spots.

Slowly, Sebastian gazed around at the apartment. The old green couch was now by the window. The table was where the armchair had been, and the armchair was where the couch used to be. In fact, everything was rearranged—and covered with plastic. It was like being inside the freezer!

"Ick!" Mrs. Jones said, as John slipped in through the door and stood staring in horror at his apartment. "That animal smells like a wet dog!"

"He *is* a wet dog, Mother," John said, chuckling. "Maybe you should've covered *him* in plastic, too."

Sebastian trotted into the kitchen. The piece of beef jerky he'd been saving for a snack was no longer between the refrigerator and the cabinet. The floor was squeaky clean. He curled his lip in

disgust. This apartment was too small for both him and Mrs. Jones.

"I'll put supper on the table," Mrs. Jones said cheerfully. "I fixed your favorite—squash, and salmon patties."

"Oh—my," John said, turning pale. "I bet you fixed tapioca for dessert, too, didn't you? Just like when I was little."

She smiled contentedly and hurried off to the kitchen.

John took Sebastian into the bathroom and rubbed his fur dry. "Don't tell on me, Sebastian, if I slip some of that stuff under the table to you."

Sebastian glared at John. It might be true that he, Sebastian the Gourmet, did have a reputation for enjoying a variety of foods. But salmon patties? Cat food? There was a limit to what he was willing to do for John! Besides, while John was eating and visiting with Mrs. Jones, he, Sebastian (Super Sleuth), had a job to do.

He gave John a sympathetic slurp across the cheek, then bolted from the bathroom, past the terrible smell in the small dining room, and through the doggie door.

Rain peppered him as he dashed through the slippery streets to La Maison Française. A dog's gotta do what a dog's gotta do (even if it means having to just grab a bite to eat on the job). His lips parted in a panting grin at the lovely thought.

Sebastian skidded to a muddy stop in front of the restaurant. Perhaps he should just slip inside with the next group of diners, blend in with their party, he thought.

The doorman looked extremely unfriendly—and big. He stomped his size 13 foot at Sebastian and yelled, "Get!"

Maybe the back door would be better, Sebastian smartly conceded. He sloshed into the alley and peered through the service door. What he needed was a disguise, something that would let him blend into the crowd, get near the professor without being recognized. His keen eyes spotted exactly what he needed. A black tuxedo, fresh from the dry cleaner's, hung nearby. The lapels were sadly out of style, but in emergencies, one must adjust.

When no one was looking, he scampered inside and wiggled into the suit. With the coat already buttoned, he could forget the troublesome cummerbund, he decided.

Now he could slip around front and come in with the other customers, perhaps get a table near—

"It's about time you got here," a man in a pale blue tuxedo snapped. "You don't seem too concerned about time, for your first night on the job."

Sebastian looked hangdog.

"Oh, never mind. The place is filling up quick and I don't have time to keep after you. Your resumé said you've been a maitre d' in some of the top spots in town, so you know what to do. Just try to divide the people up between the different waiters and keep everyone happy. Oh, and one other thing. Try to sound French."

Sebastian dogtrotted out to the reception area. And just in time!

Professor Idelmann and Marlena MacNulty Mac-Mahan arrived.

Sebastian snapped to attention and gave a little bow.

"Oh, dear," Marlena MacNulty MacMahan said. "I remember this restaurant as being quite good, but tonight the food smells like a wet dog."

"Table for two," Professor Idelmann told Sebastian.

Sebastian clenched two menus between his teeth and quickly led the professor and Marlena Mac-Nulty MacMahan to a table nearby so he could eavesdrop while he worked.

"In a corner," Marlena MacNulty MacMahan insisted. "I'm conducting an interview while we dine."

Disappointed, but undaunted, Sebastian led them

34

to a corner table. As they sat down, the professor's elbow caught the edge of Marlena MacNulty Mac-Mahan's purse and sent it to the floor with a plop.

Apologizing, the professor bent to retrieve it. But a waiter dashed over and handed it to Marlena MacNulty MacMahan. "Bonsoir, madame, monsieur. I am Maurice, your waiter."

He wrinkled his nose at Sebastian as he filled the water glasses. He told the professor and Marlena MacNulty MacMahan he'd return when they decided what to order.

The aroma of quiche Lorraine floated into the dining room, and Sebastian's nose quivered. Maurice came from the kitchen with boeuf Bordeaux for one of the tables. Sebastian drooled on his tuxedo.

The people at another table were about to divide a steak of unbelievable proportions. Sebastian whined. Oh, the things a dog must suffer to help his master!

Determined to get his mind off the delicious food, Sebastian crept closer to the table where Professor Idelmann and Marlena MacNulty MacMahan sat eating chef's salads—how could anyone eat like *rabbits* when all this good food was around?

Sebastian waited for his chance. When the professor knocked Marlena MacNulty MacMahan's purse to the floor again, Maurice made a mad dash across the room to retrieve it, nearly toppling the French pastry cart in the process. The man in the blue tuxedo came over and bawled him out. The old super sleuth used the commotion as a diversion and deftly sneaked under the table.

Hidden by the tablecloth, he listened and waited for morsels to fall to his waiting lips. If the professor was so clumsy as to knock a purse to the floor twice, he was probably clumsy enough to drop food, too. The professor was *so* clumsy, Sebastian wondered how he managed to dig up bones without shattering them.

Marlena MacNulty MacMahan shifted one shoe, nearly gouging Sebastian. He inched away, noting

in disgust how filthy her shoes were, covered in red mud. "So how did you come to dig at that particular spot for the woolly mammoth bones?" she asked.

The professor said, "I revealed my theories to the public in my book two years ago. When they all laughed at me and wouldn't buy my book, I vowed to show them all it was true. The land is owned by the city. I asked their permission to dig, and they gave it."

"You were certainly lucky to find the bones so quickly," Marlena MacNulty MacMahan said.

"It wasn't luck at all!" the professor said. "It was knowing my subject. Why, as they say, I could write a book on it!" He chuckled.

A smidgin of baked potato with chives and bacon bits fell, and Sebastian gobbled it up. (After all, as maitre d', it was his job to keep the restaurant in tiptop shape.) He listened intently as the professor and the writer talked about one of his favorite subjects—bones!

Suddenly, for the third time that night, Marlena MacNulty MacMahan's purse clunked to the floor. It landed right next to Sebastian.

The professor said. "Allow me, my dear!"

Frantically, Sebastian tried to shove the purse out from under the table, but he was too late. He found himself face to face with the professor. And, to his surprise, the professor had one hand *inside* the purse!

"Oh, dear!" the professor said. "Oh, dear!" He raised his head, bumping it on the table. Sebastian leaped up, dumping the table and spilling everything on it into the lap of Marlena MacNulty MacMahan. She shrieked something about French restaurants not being what they used to be and jumped up, bumping her head on a silver tray Maurice had brought at that same moment.

Two filets mignons rolled off the tray and to the floor. Sebastian made a dive for them, gobbling them quickly—still trying to keep the restaurant floor clean, of course.

"It's that maitre d', the dirty dog!" Maurice shouted (losing his French accent). "You ruined my service!" he yelled. "Now they probably won't even give me a tip!" Angrily he grabbed for Sebastian's throat.

Sebastian dodged Maurice, the professor, the man in the blue tuxedo (who, he decided, must be the owner) and dashed through the swinging doors to the kitchen, shedding the tuxedo (and a few globs of fur)—and managing to snatch two doggie bags as he went. He raced into the alley and into the night, relieved that it had stopped raining. He slowed down only when he could no longer hear the angry shouts from the restaurant. Panting, he collapsed into a heap and devoured the delicious doggie bags, paper and all.

The meager meal might have to last him for hours. Something told the old super sleuth that this trouble-filled night was not over yet.

5
Dog Watch Among the Bones

Sebastian's tummy rumbled. Two doggie bags were barely enough food to feed a flea—certainly not enough for a working dog.

Maybe he should go home and eat. But Sebastian remembered that salmon patties and cold squash were probably waiting in his bowl. He wanted none of that! A dog had his limits!

Maybe he should just stall until everyone was asleep and slip in through his doggie door. Then he could raid the refrigerator without anyone being the wiser.

Sebastian turned south toward Bosworthington Museum. He might as well check and see that everything was secure and that Whirter MacMahan really had locked the front door.

Of course, Whirter MacMahan claimed he only locked his key *inside*, that he'd never left the door to the museum open. How, then, could anyone get inside without breaking in? And if they did break in, why didn't it show?

Sebastian skidded to a stop and scratched behind his ear, thinking. An even better question was, *why* was someone breaking in and not stealing anything? Wasn't that why people usually broke into places? With all those rare paintings and sculptures, why didn't someone steal one?

Was this some new kind of freaky burglar who gets his kicks just leaving muddy prints? he wondered. *Red* muddy prints? Red mud, just like that on Marlena MacNulty MacMahan's shoes, he might add. Could she be the culprit?

Sebastian hastened to the museum and nudged at the front door. Locked. He checked the back door. It, too, was locked tightly. He skulked behind a prickly shrub to set up surveillance. He yawned, blinking sleepily. Well, the dog watch must be better than eating salmon and squash.

Mist settled over the ground. Clouds scudded across the moon. Sebastian's nose quivered. A human was nearby. A dark figure lurked around the front door. Someone inserted a key and opened the door!

Sebastian squinted at the figure. Was it Whirter MacMahan? Or Marlena MacNulty MacMahan?

They were the only ones with keys. Or was there a third key that no one knew about?

The old super sleuth dashed toward the door, hoping to slip through before it latched shut behind the intruder. *Whomp!* The door collided with his nose. He was too late.

Peering through the door glass he could see the dark figure skulking toward the far wing, the one with the prehistoric exhibits. The intruder—was it Whirter MacMahan, or maybe Marlena MacNulty MacMahan?—carried boxes. Was the burglar planning on filling the boxes? With what? Paintings? Sculptures?

Sebastian remembered the museum skylights. If only he could get to the roof, perhaps he could see who was inside and what he—or she—was doing. He scurried around the side to the fire escape and edged his way up the metal steps. His stomach churned. Heights were not his favorite places—after all, he wasn't a bird dog. He forced himself to keep climbing and not look down.

When he reached the roof, Sebastian breathed a relieved sigh. He'd made it! He bellied up to the skylight and peered down.

The dark figure was near the woolly mammoth. Long boxes, like the one the professor used to store the bone in, were spread around the floor. Was someone stealing the woolly mammoth? But the boxes were not that large. Maybe *part* of the woolly mammoth?

How could he stop the theft? If only he could successfully dial the 911 emergency number! But those tiny push buttons were not made for his huge paws. Even if he could get the number, he'd probably never be able to make the police understand. Humans could be so *dense* sometimes!

While Sebastian debated his next step, the dark figure crept away with the boxes under his arm—or was it *her* arm? Sebastian gritted his teeth and started the tedious climb back down the fire escape. Going down was so much harder! It was most uncomfortable to see the ground so far below.

By the time he got around to the front door again, the prowler was gone, vanished into the mist.

The chagrined canine trotted home and raided

the refrigerator, stuffing himself in consolation before falling into a troubled sleep (on the *floor*, as he'd feared).

First thing the next day, while John and his mother still slept, Sebastian searched the house for a proper disguise. He had to get back into the museum. There was Mrs. Jones' hat that looked like a bowl of flowers. And there was her fur coat. As tasteless as they were, they'd have to do!

Sebastian shrugged into them, then hastened to the Bosworthington Museum. By now Whirter Mac-Mahan would have discovered the missing woolly mammoth (unless, of course, he himself was the culprit). Maybe he, Sebastian (Super Sleuth), could make someone understand what had happened last night.

In his cunning disguise he slipped right past the guards. Blending in adeptly with the crowd of museum visitors, Sebastian browsed his way into the prehistoric exhibit. There he skidded to a halt, staring.

There was the woolly mammoth—intact. Every bone in place.

6
Every Dog Has His Day

Sebastian stood gaping at the skeleton of the woolly mammoth. Had the old super sleuth's eyes been deceiving him last night? (Was it something he ate?) Was his career as a clever canine detective coming to a close? Ended because of failing eyesight?

No! he answered himself. He *did* see someone sneaking around the museum, with boxes in hand and crime in mind.

It had appeared that the cat burglar was stealing the skeleton of the woolly mammoth. But since the woolly mammoth was still here, what, then, *did* the burglar take last night?

Sebastian touched his cold, moist nose to the skeleton. The leg bone smelled funny, like the little statue of a poodle John won at the amusement park by hitting a target with tennis balls.

He sniffed some of the other bones. Some of them smelled funny, too. And they did not seem quite the same color as the others—maybe a tiny bit whiter. He searched his computerlike mind—plaster! Plaster of paris—that was what the bones smelled like. He ran his pink tongue along one of them. It tasted odd, too.

"Hey, lady!" a guard yelled. "Don't do that! Are you weird or something?"

Sebastian turned on his heels and ran. He had learned all he needed to know.

He dashed down the hall and to the front door of the museum, pushing it open with both paws. He almost stumbled into John's arms!

"Excuse me, ma'am," John said, holding the door open for Sebastian.

Sebastian gave a quick, polite nod, then dashed down the steps and cut across the Bosworthington Museum lawn to John's car. He shed the disguise, then dashed down the street as fast as he could push his paws against the pavement. He, Sebastian (Super Sleuth), was positive he had the solution now.

All he had to do was prove his theory and let John take care of the arrest. Toward the outskirts of town he ran. Finally he saw his destination—Professor Idelmann's dig.

The reporters had gathered with their notepads and cameras once more. And once more the professor was pacing up and down, giving another of his pompous lectures.

The cameras ground away. The "Afternoon Live" news team was there. So much the better, Sebastian thought. He'd prove his theory and the whole city would see it—live.

The professor's expression changed as Sebastian raced toward him. "That dog! Not again! Stop that dog!" he shouted, throwing a small shovel at Sebastian.

"An unidentified dog has invaded the prehistoric dig of Professor Idelmann," the newswoman shouted into the mike. "This is all live, folks. Right here on Channel 11."

Sebastian dodged the shovel and leaped into the hole with the professor as every camera and every microphone was aimed his way. *Scritch, scratch—* his paws dug at the loose red dirt, and Professor Idelmann tugged at him, shouting things no good doggie would repeat.

Sebastian struck something hard. He snapped his teeth around it and extracted a bone covered with red dirt.

"Stop, you stupid animal!" Professor Idelmann shouted. "Stop!"

Sebastian leaped from the hole and raced off toward the center of the city. Professor Idelmann was right behind him, shouting ugly names and waving a trowel. And behind him came the camera crew and reporters with their heavy gear, struggling to keep up.

The old super sleuth was tiring—what he needed was an energy snack. But he dared not stop. He had to get the bone to John. Then he spotted John's car racing toward them.

It screeched to a halt and John leaped out. "I'm so sorry, Professor Idelmann! I saw what happened on the television in Whirter MacMahan's office. I came as soon as I could. I—Sebastian, stop!"

Sebastian carried the bone over to John, then slumped onto his belly with the bone between his paws. Now to prove his theory. He swiped his pink tongue along the ends of the bone. Tiny holes—and numbers! He was right. Now, if only he could make John see them, too, and understand. If only there weren't such a language barrier between them!

7
A Bone to Pick

John pulled the bone from Sebastian. "I'm so sorry, Professor," he said, handing it to the professor. "It won't happen agai—hey, wait a minute."

Sebastian pressed his cold nose to John's hand, encouraging him to go on.

John pulled the bone back. He ran his finger on the bone. "This bone has little holes drilled in the ends—just like the ones at the museum! And—" He turned the bone over. "It has a number on it—this is a marked bone!"

Sebastian breathed a sigh of relief. Now John knew what he, Sebastian (Super Sleuth), had figured out. The professor had been slowly raiding the museum of its woolly mammoth skeleton and replacing it with phony bones. He was using an old discovery to try and make people think that the area was a burial ground for woolly mammoths, just as he'd claimed in his book.

"Empty your pockets, please," John said.

The dejected professor did. And right there, with a collection of string, an empty wallet, and an old Cracker Jack prize, was Marlena MacNulty MacMahan's key. The professor must've stolen it last night when he knocked her purse to the floor. He probably had it at the dig that day, too. That was why he got Marlena MacNulty MacMahan's purse for her—it gave him a chance to replace the key.

John arrested the professor on live television while Sebastian posed for the cameras, his paw securely on the bone.

Whirter MacMahan was really surprised when he got his bones back. He didn't even know they were missing.

Chief grudgingly complimented John on the good job. "If it weren't for the superhorrendous appetite of that conniving canine of yours," Chief told John, "I guess this whole thing would have gone unnoticed."

Sebastian curled his lip. Is that what Chief thought it was? A case of accidental appetite? Couldn't Chief recognize good detective work when he saw it?

Sebastian padded out to the car in an indignant huff. Would the world never recognize his true worth? Was he, Sebastian (Super Sleuth), destined to be just another pretty dog to them?

John climbed into the car. "If it weren't for you, old boy, we'd never have known we had more than a midnight prowler."

Sebastian panted a grin. At last, someone who saw him for his fantastic detective work.

"Yessir, you greedy old thing, if you hadn't dug up that bone, I'd have never had the chance to see the numbers and assembly holes on it and crack this case."

A low rumble vibrated Sebastian's throat. Even *you*, John?

"You ought to appreciate the leftovers tonight, old fellow," John said, turning onto their street. "It's Mother's last night here, and she's fixing roast beef with all the trimmings."

Roast beef and *she's* leaving. That was two good pieces of news, Sebastian figured, cheering up some.

Sure enough, the most sumptuous smells drifted from the apartment as they drove up.

Sebastian's tummy growled hungrily as they strolled in to greet Mrs. Jones—and a lady?

"This is Maude Culpepper," Mrs. Jones said, giving John a little shove toward the woman. "I just know you two are going to hit it off wonderfully."

Maude Culpepper, who was a lot prettier than her name, fluttered her lashes at John, smiling.

Sebastian's throat rumbled.

"Well, hi!" John said. "You aren't at all what I expected—I mean, Mother and I don't ordinarily have the same tastes, I mean—" John flushed.

Maude Culpepper's laughter sounded like tinkling crystal. She stuck out her hand in greeting. "I admit I was a bit nervous about you, too."

"And look, John," Mrs. Jones said. "I told her you wouldn't mind, all things considered. She brought Lady Sharon with her."

"Oh, wow! An Old English Sheepdog!" John said. "Look, Sebastian. Say hello to Lady Sharon."

Lady Sharon wagged the stump of her tail eagerly. She touched her cool, moist nose to his in greeting. A whiff of *Ode de Doggie* greeted his sensitive nose.

Why she could be on the cover of *Your Dog* magazine any day! the cosmopolitan canine realized.

Cautiously the quick-witted Sebastian backed toward the doggie door.

He knew what Mrs. Jones was trying to do— tempt him and John out of happy bachelorhood! Well, no thank you!

In one swift move, he bolted through the flap of his doggie door and ran out into the night.

In the alley, the old super sleuth stood up on the neighbors' garbage can and sniffed. Tacos and hot sauce. Good enough. He felt like eating out tonight, anyway.

Why didn't John come on out, too? Was he just being polite? Of course, he, Sebastian (Super Sleuth), always reacted much faster than John. John, after all, was only human. He didn't solve mysteries as fast and he didn't escape ladies as fast, either.

Sebastian figured that Maude Culpepper was all right, for a human, but John shouldn't smile and look at her like that. She was liable to think he was *serious!* And of course, he *couldn't* be serious—could he? Certainly not! Sebastian assured himself.

He sighed, thinking of the sweet aroma of *Ode de Doggie* perfume. He realized with a modest blush that Lady Sharon had been instantly attracted to the incomparable canine—his dashing ways and rugged good looks. What dog in her right mind wouldn't be?

But it was best not to encourage her.

In the long run, he'd only wind up breaking her heart. He, after all, was married to his work. The stump of his tail wiggled as the hairy hawkshaw anticipated his next exciting mystery.

He scavenged up the remains of an apple pie—the perfect dessert when dining out.

ABOUT THE AUTHOR

MARY BLOUNT CHRISTIAN is the author of dozens of children's books, including two previous Sebastian books, *Sebastian (Super Sleuth) and the Hair of the Dog Mystery* and *Sebastian (Super Sleuth) and the Crummy Yummies Caper.* She is creator and moderator of the PBS-TV series "Children's Bookshelf," and teaches college writing courses in Houston, Texas, where she lives.

ABOUT THE ILLUSTRATOR

LISA MCCUE is a talented new illustrator who lives in Tappan, New York.